For Dad, a scientist at heart
— S.W.
For Paul — D.O'C.

Creature Teacher Science Shocker is published by Stone Arch Books,
A Capstone Imprint
1710 Roe Crest Drive
North Mankato, Minnesota 56003
www.mycapstone.com

Creature Teacher Science Shocker was originally published in English in 2015. This
translation is published by arrangement with Oxford University Press.

Library of Congress Cataloging-in-Publication Data is available
on the Library of Congress website.

ISBN: 978-1-4965-5705-6 (Library Binding)
ISBN: 978-1-4965-5689-9 (Paperback)
ISBN: 978-1-4965-5709-4 (eBook PDF)

Summary:
One creature is hard enough to handle. But two? That's double trouble! Jake's class is
competing in the Whiz-BANG Science Fair and there is just one thing standing between
them and success . . . Creature! And Creature's made a friend! With two mischievous
little monsters causing havoc, things are about to get explosive!

Designer:
Mackenzie Lopez

Printed in Canada.
010407F17

By Sam Watkins Illustrated by David O'Connell

CREATURE TEACHER

Science Shocker

STONE ARCH BOOKS
a capstone imprint

TABLE OF CONTENTS

CHAPTER 1:

HAVE YOU GOT A TISSUE?

"Hi! Welcome to the Whiz-BANG Science Fair!"

A girl in a T-shirt with a lightning bolt on it shoved a flyer into Jake's hand.

"Err . . . thanks," he mumbled as she disappeared into the crowd.

Jake stuffed the flyer into his pocket, took a deep breath, and began to walk across the lobby of the Natural History Museum. He was late. He should have been here an hour ago to help set up the Class 5B exhibit. Now it was ten o'clock, the fair had opened, and the museum lobby was jam-packed with excited people, all jostling to get into the main hall.

Something whacked his elbow.

"Excuse me, Goliath bird-eating spider coming through!"

"Sorry . . ." Jake backed away as a boy squeezed past, carrying a large glass tank. Inside, he saw a brown, hairy spider the size of a small rat.

"You can pet her if you want," the boy said. "She doesn't bite . . . normally."

Jake was saved by a shout.

"JAKE — over here!"

His friend Nora was standing by the doorway to the main hall. With her were two more of his classmates, Karl and Barnaby. He wriggled through the sea of bodies to them.

"Where have you been?" Nora grumbled. "It's only two hours till the judging."

"Sorry. Connie decided to play a game of hide-and-seek as we were leaving."

Nora rolled her eyes. "Haven't you told your sister how very important this competition is?"

"I tried, but she's silly. She just stuck her diaper on her head," Jake said.

Barnaby's eyes widened and he nudged Jake. "Speaking of silly . . ."

Jake turned to see the tall figure of their teacher, Mr. Hyde, bobbing through the crowd in a very happy mood. He was wearing a white lab coat, khaki shorts, purple socks, and sandals.

Karl chuckled.

Nora frowned. "Don't be mean toward Mr. Hyde."

Jake nodded, although Barnaby did sort of have a point. Mr. Hyde didn't look exactly normal. But then again, Mr. Hyde *wasn't* normal — he was extraordinary. He was

officially the best teacher in the universe.
But he did have one teeny, tiny, humongous
problem . . .

"We'll have to keep an eye on Mr. Hyde
today," Jake muttered to his friends.
"Imagine the chaos if he turned into Creature
in here."

Nora nodded, then put her finger to her
lips as Mr. Hyde bounced up.

"There you are, Class 5B whiz kids!" he
cried. "Are you ready for the Whiz-BANG
Brainiest Whiz Kid Competition? We can
win, you know — I've got a nose for these
things! Come along. Alexis and Woodstock
are waiting."

As Mr. Hyde hustled the students into
the main hall, Jake was surrounded by a
dizzying blend of bangs, flashes, and smells.
Everywhere, tables were piled high with

chemical mixtures and electronic gadgets. In the center of the hall, a gigantic volcano belched out fumes every few seconds.

Mr. Hyde marched off, with Jake and his friends scurrying along behind. As they rounded the volcano, Jake stopped.

Mrs. Blunt, their principal, was standing a few feet away.

Jake felt a pang of guilt, even though he'd done nothing wrong. Mrs. Blunt had that effect on you. She was standing guard over a large object covered in a sheet.

"Class 5A's exhibit," Nora whispered.

"What is it?" Jake asked in a low voice. "They've kept it really quiet."

"Whatever it is, it's not working," Nora said. "Amelia was yelling some *very* rude things at it earlier."

Everyone giggled. Amelia Trotter-Hogg, also known as the most annoying person in the universe, was always trying to cause trouble for them, but Mrs. Blunt thought she was a package of ponytailed perfection.

Mrs. Blunt's guilt-inducing glare had no effect on Mr. Hyde.

"Morning, Mrs. Blunt!" he sang, breezing past the frowning principal. Jake shuffled away, looking at the floor. He could feel her laser eyes boring holes in his skull.

"Oh, look," he heard Nora say. "Someone's taken the stand next to ours. It was empty earlier."

Jake peered at the sign. *ANT ANTICS.* Hey, Nora, you like bugs . . . Nora?"

Nora had shot behind him, a look of horror on her face.

"Keep walking," she muttered, head down, clinging to his arm. Jake looked over as they passed the Ant Antics stand, curious to see what had freaked Nora out. A frizzy-haired boy with glasses was standing at a table, talking loudly to a group of children.

"Hurry!" Nora cried, pushing Jake toward their stand. In front of them, Mr. Hyde stopped and clapped his hands, beaming.

"There she blows!"

Jake grinned. Their exhibit was pretty cool.

It was officially called "Have You Got a Tissue?" At least that's what Nora called it. Everyone else called it the "Giant Nose." Or just "The Nose."

The Nose was mainly Nora's idea. It was built from papier-mâché and was the size of a kid's playhouse. When you pulled a lever on the side, a bucket-load of purple snot sneezed out of the nostrils. Nora liked the fact that it demonstrated the workings of the human immune system. Everyone else just liked the fact that it was a giant nose.

Woodstock and Alexis were putting some finishing touches on The Nose as Nora sped past it and stood fuming with outrage next to it.

"Whoa!" exclaimed Woodstock, nearly dropping his paint.

Jake peeked around. "What's up, Nora?"

"The boy on the Ant Antics stand!" Nora said through gritted teeth. "It's that dreadful know-it-all, Isaac Einstein. He thinks he knows everything there is to know about bugs. How ridiculous is that?"

"Totally ridiculous," Jake agreed.

"Imagine if he wins . . ." Nora groaned.

"He won't, because *we're* going to win," Alexis declared. "Our exhibit is educational and fun. Isn't it, Nora?"

"I like your thinking, Alexis!" Mr. Hyde's head popped out from around The Nose. "WHAT ARE WE, FOLKS?" he cheered.

"Winners," mumbled everyone.

"Louder!" cried Mr. Hyde.

"WINNERS!" they all shouted.

BEEEEEEEEEE–E–E–E–E–E–P!

A foghorn-like beep rattled Jake's eardrums. Something cold and metallic gripped his arm and swiveled him around.

Jake blinked twice. "What on earth?"

CHAPTER 2:

RULE BOT

A robot was standing in front of Jake. The front of its head was a screen, on which was displayed a very grumpy face. A flashing blue police siren sat on its head.

Before Jake could move, a sticker popped out of a slot in the robot's tummy. The robot shot a metal arm out, grabbed the sticker, and slapped it on Jake's forehead.

"A Sad Face!" exclaimed Karl.

"What?" Jake peeled the sticker off. It was, indeed, one of Mrs. Blunt's Sad Face stickers. Sad Face stickers were given to students who broke the school rules. If you got three Sad Faces, you had to work on Mrs. Blunt's Rockery, shifting heavy rocks.

"VIOLATION OF RULE 63 — NO SHOUTING!" the robot barked, sounding suspiciously like an electronic Mrs. Blunt.

"It must be 5A's project!" Nora cried. "It's working now!"

Woodstock groaned. "So that's what the old dragon's been hiding — HEY!"

The robot had planted a sticker on Woodstock's chest.

"VIOLATION OF RULE 27 — NEVER CALL THE PRINCIPAL AN OLD DRAGON," the robot rasped.

Barnaby snorted, and got a sticker for violation of Rule 41 — No Snorting.

Mr. Hyde scratched his head.

"Well, it's very impressive, if a tad overenthusiastic," he said. "I'd never have thought Class 5A would be so good at robotics. Listen up, guys, I'm going to grab a coffee. I'll be back in a jiffy." He strode off.

"NEWT! I thought I saw you walk past!" came a loud, nasally voice.

Nora ducked, but she was too late. The frizzy-haired boy from the Ant Antics stand was peering around The Nose.

"My name is *Nora*," the girl growled.

"Oh yes. Sorry, I never remember first names." Isaac squinted at The Nose through his thick glasses. "So, what exactly is this?"

"It's a nose," Nora said darkly.

"Ah." Isaac walked around The Nose. He pointed to the lever. "What's that?"

"That is what is known as a lever."

"I know, but what does it *do*?" he asked.

Nora put two buckets under the nostrils. "Pull it."

"Aaaaaaaaaa-CHOO!"

Two waterfalls of gross purple snot exploded out of the nostrils into the buckets.

Isaac dipped his finger in.

"Purple. I hypothesize . . . potassium permanganate?"

Nora looked smug. "Wrong. It's sugar, flour, and water. And purple food dye."

"I hate to say this, Newt — but snot is green, not purple. It all has to do with the neutrophils. What happens is —"

Nora crossed her arms. "You don't have to explain. I know everything about noses. As for the color, well, Woodstock was in charge of the snot, and he wanted purple."

"It's more . . . artistic," Woodstock mumbled, looking guiltily at Nora.

Isaac was bending down to peer up a nostril when Alexis hissed. "*Psst*, here comes trouble . . ."

"Now THAT is the DUMBEST thing I've ever seen."

Jake groaned. Amelia Trotter-Hogg, most annoying person in the universe, was standing smirking at him. Behind her hovered her two only slightly less annoying friends.

"What *is* that thing?" Amelia asked. "Wait, I know. It's a Pile of Garbage."

This was obviously the funniest joke ever, judging by the screeches of laughter from Amelia's friends.

Amelia looked at Barnaby's Sad Face sticker and snickered.

"I see our brilliant Rule-Bot got *you* already, McCrumb," she said.

Barnaby pulled the sticker off, annoyed.

"Rule-Bot? Is that its name? Pain-in-the-Bot, more like . . ."

Amelia shrugged. "Say what you want. *We're* going to win the competition. You won't be so rude then, because we'll be on the *Rise and Shine* TV Show, and Mrs. Blunt says we'll be famous, and —"

"Mrs. *Blunt* said that?" Nora exploded. "Is being famous all she cares about? The best part of the prize is a day at Space Cadet School. That's way better than being on TV!"

"Huh, you *would* think that, boring Nora."

"Hello, what's going on?" Mr. Hyde had reappeared. He stepped between Amelia and Nora. "It's good to be competitive, but can we do it in a friendly way?"

Amelia frowned.

"Fine. Good luck, Class 5B," she said. "You're going to need it," she then mouthed at Jake so Mr. Hyde couldn't hear.

"That's more like it," Mr. Hyde said. "Can we return the gesture, 5B?"

There was a tense silence. With an effort, Nora spoke.

"Amelia, your robot is . . . interesting. Do tell me how you made it."

Amelia looked shifty. "Oh, bits of computers — that sort of thing . . ."

"How does it talk?" Karl asked.

Amelia shrugged. "I dunno. I didn't work on that part."

Jake leaned forward. "Who did?"

"That was the Profess—"

"Shh!" one of her friends hissed. Amelia put her hand over her mouth.

"Profess . . . Professor?" said Jake, slowly.
"Hang on . . ."

Amelia's eyes darted around like a
cornered animal. She started to back away,
talking at top speed.

"What does it matter, because we're going to win and be on TV and we'll be celebrities and rich and . . . oh, I've had enough of this. Come on, Rule-Bot, let's leave these Class 5B bores to their stupid snot machine," she snapped. Her two friends reattached themselves to her sides and they stalked off, followed by a whirring Rule-Bot.

Jake's cheeks felt hot. He turned to the others. "Did you hear that part about a professor?"

Woodstock looked grim. "They got someone to make their robot."

"That's against the rules!" Alexis exclaimed. "The students have to make the exhibits themselves. Don't they, sir?"

"Well, yes," Mr. Hyde said. "But we don't have any proof — let's not jump to conclusions."

"They cheated," Karl said.

"They used a professor," Nora said.

"An EVIL professor, I bet," Woodstock added, his bangs shaking.

"OK, that's enough," Mr. Hyde declared, becoming more and more uncomfortable. "I'll look into it. Perhaps we should check out some of the other competitors, huh? See what we're up against. I vote we stop next door to Isaac's stand. I'm dying to see what antics these ants are up to!"

CHAPTER 3:

MAKE SPARKS FLY

Alexis, Karl, and Barnaby decided to stay at The Nose while the rest of them trailed off to see Isaac's exhibit.

Jake's mind raced. Class 5A had *clearly* cheated. Mrs. Blunt was so desperate to be famous she'd do anything to win! *But Mr. Hyde's right — we don't have any proof.*

"Now *that's* what I call science!" Isaac's voice interrupted Jake's thoughts.

The Ant Antics table was in front of them. On it sat a huge glass tank, filled with dirt. As Jake looked closer he saw a maze of tunnels running through the dirt, with black specks shuffling along them.

"This is our formicarium," declared Isaac. "It's an ant farm with approximately ten thousand ants." He poked Nora. "Newt, remember last year when I beat you by one question in the quiz because you didn't know what a formicarium was?"

"I wouldn't have known that, either," said Mr. Hyde quickly, as Nora's glasses began to steam up. "Interesting display. Fascinati . . ."

His voice trailed off.

"Hello! So many bright young scientists here today!"

A woman with glasses and a bubbling mass of red, curly hair had popped up behind the formicarium. Jake couldn't help noticing that she had planets dangling from her ears.

Nora stared at her. "Ooh, I love your earrings. Saturn's my favorite planet."

The woman's eyes twinkled. "Mine too!" She turned to Mr. Hyde. "I'm Miss Jex, Isaac's teacher. And you are . . . ?"

Mr. Hyde's mouth opened, then shut.

"Mr. Hyde," Woodstock said helpfully.

"Lovely to meet you! What's your exhibit?" Miss Jex looked at Mr. Hyde again.

He made a gagging noise. "Haaav . . . haaaaaav . . . Have You Got a Tissue!"

"Bless you!" Miss Jex said. "It is a bit fumy in here!" She handed him a tissue from her pocket. Mr. Hyde looked at it blankly.

"Jee . . . per?"

Jeeper?! With a jolt, Jake realized that his teacher's face had turned pink. Mr. Hyde was changing! *He's all flustered because he thinks Isaac's exhibit is way better than ours! We have to get him out of here . . .*

He poked Nora, who was still staring at Miss Jex. "Look, her eyes are different colors," she whispered. "One's blue and one's green, they're amazing!"

"Stop looking at Miss Jex and look at Mr. Hyde — he's changing!" Jake whispered back. Louder, he said, "We should go back to our stand, sir . . ."

"Ooh, can I come?" Miss Jex asked.

Jake bit his lip. *We have to get Mr. Hyde on his own!*

"Shouldn't you stay here, to, um . . . feed your ants?" he said. "They look hungry . . ."

"Isaac can look after the ants, can't you dear? Come on, I'm dying to see your stand!"

Miss Jex began pulling Mr. Hyde away, chattering non-stop.

". . . can't wait for the judging . . . SO excited about Space Cadet School!" Jake, Nora, and Woodstock trailed along behind, giving each other anxious looks. "And the space shuttle trip sounds FANTASTIC, doesn't it?"

Mr. Hyde found his voice. "What . . . what space shuttle trip?"

"The space shuttle simulator at Space Cadet School," said Miss Jex. "You get to go into orbit and see Earth from 155 miles away!"

Mr. Hyde's face went from shocking pink to ghastly green.

"I'm afraid that sounds terrifying to me," he mumbled. "I'm scared of heights."

"Well, that's too bad!" Miss Jex patted his arm. "Well, I hear they've got these amazing zero gravity toilets . . . OOH!"

Miss Jex pointed excitedly to a nearby table. A sign on it read *MAKE SPARKS FLY!* On the table was a large metal globe on a pole. A girl was fiddling with it.

"A Van de Graaff generator! When you touch the globe, the static electricity makes your hair stand on end. Come on . . ."

She pulled Mr. Hyde across to the table.

"Can we try it?" Miss Jex asked.

"It's not working," the girl said. "I've changed the wires, but nothing's happening."

Slowly, Miss Jex placed her hand on the globe. Nothing happened. She peered at the wires. "Positive, negative. Hmm, seems OK."

Mr. Hyde coughed and straightened his tie.

"Let me see, Miss Jex," he said in an oddly deep voice. "I know about these things . . ."

Mr. Hyde leaned over, putting his hand out to steady himself on the table.

His hand missed. He fell forward, grabbing the metal globe as he did so.

CRRRRRRRRRRAAAAAACK!

A sizzling shower of sparks flew out of the globe!

Both teachers' hair stood on end like two excited dandelion puffs. Mr. Hyde's eyes crossed, and Miss Jex's earrings spun round and round.

Bzzzzzzzzzzzzzzzzzzzzz–z–z–z–z . . .

"TURN IT OFF!" yelled Woodstock.

The girl behind the table clicked a switch frantically. "I can't!"

"Pull their hands away!" shouted Nora.

Jake felt a shock run up his arm as he grabbed Mr. Hyde's hand and yanked it off the globe. Nora did the same with Miss Jex.

Bzzz . . . zzz . . . ZWUP.

A crackle. Then silence.

Phew, Jake thought, rubbing his arm. He looked around. A crowd had gathered, all staring curiously at the two teachers' frizzed-up hair.

Miss Jex took off her glasses.

"That shock must have done something to my eyes," she said, blinking. "Mr. Hyde, you are positively glowing!"

"Uh-oh," Woodstock murmured.

Mr. Hyde was bathed in a shimmering orange glow. A strong smell of burning rubber wafted into Jake's nostrils . . .

He's changing into Creature, Jake realized.

"BACK TO THE NOSE!" He grabbed one of Mr. Hyde's arms. Nora grabbed the other.

"Make way! Electric-shock victim coming through!" Woodstock shouted.

The crowd parted as they pulled Mr. Hyde to their stand, skidded up to The Nose, and shoved the glowing teacher behind it.

Then came a bright flash of light.

AAAAAAAAAAAAARRRRRT!

Wheeeeeeee · · · · · · · · · ·

POP! POP! POP!

BANG!

CHAPTER 4:

FUN WITH FROG SPAWN

For a few seconds, Jake couldn't see anything through the billowing cloud of purple smoke. Then he began to make out a shadowy figure through the haze.

"Mr. Hyde?" he called. "I mean, Creature? Is that you?"

"No, it's me." Woodstock emerged from the smoke, coughing.

As the smoke cleared, two more shadowy figures turned into Nora and Barnaby. Creature was nowhere to be seen.

Alexis and Karl emerged from the smoke.

"What happened? Did something explode?" Alexis asked.

"Mr. Hyde changed again," Jake sighed.

Karl groaned. "Oh man, where is he?"

"I don't know," Jake said. "But we have to catch him." He paused as he stared around him. "Hey, what's happening?"

A crowd of excited people had gathered in front of The Nose, talking loudly.

"What was that bang?"

"Cool — an exploding nose!"

"Can you make it explode again?"

"Um," Jake and his friends looked at each other, confused by the flood of questions.

"Let me through! Newt! What's going on?"

A red-faced Isaac stomped toward them.

"What was that explosion?" he squawked. "I was giving a charming presentation on the digestive systems of ants when my whole audience disappeared!"

"Oh. Well, sorry about that," mumbled Jake, trying to sidestep around him. Isaac blocked Jake's path.

"And where on earth is Miss Jex?" he demanded. "The judging is starting soon! She really should be at the stand!"

Behind Jake, Nora inhaled sharply. "The judging is starting soon? What are we going to do?"

"Don't worry about the judging now," Jake whispered, calling his friends over. "We've got to find Creature."

"So what are we waiting for?" Alexis whispered. "Let's go!"

"What are you whispering about?" Isaac asked, poking Nora on the arm. "And *where* is Miss Jex?"

"I don't know, Isaac," Nora said. "She was here a minute ago! Maybe she went to get a coffee? Teachers love coffee. Now please leave us alone."

Isaac stomped off, muttering under his breath.

"Finally!" Jake said, relieved. "All right. We need two people to stay at the stand to deal with all these people. The rest of us will look for Creature."

"I'll stay," Karl offered. "I'm good at crowd control."

"I'll stay too," Woodstock said.

"OK," Jake said. "Nora, Alexis, let's go."

"How about me?" Barnaby asked.

"You can't come," Nora said.

Barnaby glared. "Why not?"

"Because you're a troublemaker."

"Am not," fussed Barnaby.

"Yes, you are!" Nora insisted.

Jake ground his teeth. "We don't have time for this! Okay Barnaby, you can come with us if you promise not to cause trouble."

He paused. In the corner of his eye he caught a flash of blue light. The curved shape of Rule-Bot was gliding toward them through the crowd. *How could they look for Creature with Rule-Bot hovering around?*

Jake had a sudden brainwave.

"On second thought," he said to Barnaby. "Start causing trouble!"

Barnaby stared. "What?"

"Rule-Bot's coming this way. Distract him away from us!"

"How?" Barnaby was confused.

"Just do what you're good at, Barnaby! He'll follow you and leave us free to find Creature."

Barnaby's eyes gleamed. "Cool! I can definitely do that."

He ducked under the table and walked toward the approaching Rule-Bot. He stopped just in front of the robot and said something that Jake couldn't hear, but Rule-Bot could.

"BEEEEEEEEEP!"

The face on Rule-Bot's screen went from slightly sad to flaming furious in a matter of seconds! Jake saw one, two, no, *three* Sad Face stickers shoot out of Rule-Bot's small tummy slot.

Barnaby wasn't about to get stickered again. He leapfrogged over the robot and shot off across the hall, laughing.

Rule-Bot spun around and gave chase, its siren wailing and light flashing like a police car on a chase.

"I wonder what Barnaby said?" Alexis grinned.

Jake shrugged. "It worked, whatever it was! Come on."

He started to push through the crowd of students swarming around their still-fumy Nose stand

Explosions were firing off from all sorts of stands, and clouds of evil-smelling, colored smoke were filling the room. It was overwhelming! A loud bang from a nearby stand made Jake and his friends jump. They turned to see what had happened.

"Our explosion was better than yours!" shouted a boy from the stand, seeing Jake and the others looking.

Jake frowned. "I think we've started some sort of explosion competition," he muttered to Alexis and Nora.

Just then they had to dodge out of the way of an annoyed-looking museum worker. She was charging across the hall, shaking her head and yelling at everyone to stop blowing things up.

"At least no one will see Creature in this smoke," Alexis said, as another disgusting cloud surrounded them.

"Yeah, but neither will we." Jake waved the smoke away.

Nora nudged Jake's arm. "Hey! Look over there! Under that table!" Jake's gaze followed the line of Nora's pointing finger.

Everyone peered through the haze. Just ahead, a teacher was carefully placing large glass jars on a table.

Underneath the table, Jake spotted
the familiar furry shape of Creature with
his head of black hair and a large pair of
glasses perched on his nose. He was holding
something up to his mouth.

Jake, Nora, and Alexis crouched down to get a better look.

"What's he got?" Jake whispered, creeping closer.

"Looks like a jar of clear jelly," Nora said.

At that moment, the teacher placed a cardboard sign on the front of the table.

Jake looked at the sign:

They all looked at each other. "That's not jelly," said Alexis.

"It's FROG SPAWN!" squeaked Nora.

"Stop him!" Jake cried.

All three of them made a dash for the table.

Creature opened his mouth wide and tipped the slimy contents of the jar into it.

CHAPTER 5:

CLONING AROUND

Jake, Alexis, and Nora froze, as Creature swallowed the frog spawn in one gulp. A look of great surprise came over his face.

"HIC!" Creature shot into the air.

THUNK. His head whacked the underside of the table, making all the jars jump. The teacher on the stand stared at them.

"Funny! The frog spawn is lively today," he said. But then an explosion on the next stand sent the teacher diving for cover.

Jake crept forward. "Now is our chance."

He stopped.

What was happening to Creature? His legs were getting longer . . . skinnier . . . and greener . . . till they almost looked like . . . *frog's legs?*

"R-r-r-ribbit?" Creature croaked, taking an experimental hop. "Rrrribbit!"

"He's turned into a frog!" Alexis squeaked.

Nora shook her head. "Only his bottom half! He's half-frog, half-Creature. The electric shock must have done something to his molecules —"

BANG!

The biggest explosion yet ripped through the hall, followed by a mushroom cloud of smelly green smoke. With a croak, Creature rocketed out from under the table and took a wild leap on his froggy legs, straight over Jake's head.

"After him!" Alexis cried.

Jake and his friends chased after Creature. Most people seemed to be making a dash for the main entrance to escape the smoke, but Creature didn't seem bothered by it.

Creature hopped the other way from the crowd and disappeared into the smoke. Taking a deep breath, Jake plunged in after him. Smoke filled his eyes, making them water. *Where'd he go?* Aha, just ahead! A glimpse of a bright green bottom . . .

"This way," Jake shouted to Nora and Alexis. He emerged from the fog to see Creature hop up onto a table covered in plants. No one was at the stand — everyone had made a dash for the doors.

A sign on the table read *PLANT POWER*, and a pot of marigolds sat in the middle. Creature stared at the marigolds.

Jake, Nora, and Alexis tiptoed closer, waiting for their chance to pounce.

Up closer, Jake could see why Creature was so fixated on the flowers. A shiny green fly was buzzing around them.

Creature's back legs tensed, ready to spring on the fly. Jake froze, ready to spring on Creature.

"Jeeperrrrr?"

Creature staggered back in surprise and almost fell off the table. Another furry face was rising up on the other side of the flowers.

Jake gasped.

Another Creature was gazing at Creature through the marigolds!

PLANT
POWER

Jake stared at the new Creature. It cocked its head to one side. At the same time, Creature did the same. It cocked its head the other way. Creature did too. It was almost like they were looking at themselves in a mirror. They were alike even down to their glasses! The only difference was their hair. Creature had black hair. The new Creature had a fluff of red hair.

"Has Creature been cloned?" Nora asked. "I saw an exhibit called *Cloning Around*."

"But their hair is different," Jake said. "Aren't clones supposed to be identical?"

Nora shrugged. "Yes, normally, but maybe they haven't quite perfected their cloning technique yet."

Creature suddenly leaned forward, picked a marigold from the flowerpot, and held it out to the new Creature.

"Eeee?" The new Creature looked at the flower just as the fly decided to land on it.

KER-SNAP! In less than a millisecond, a long, pink frog-like tongue shot out of Creature's mouth, curled around the unlucky fly, and drew it back into his mouth. It was so quick, the new Creature didn't even seem to notice. It reached out its hand for the flower.

Creature opened his mouth and his tongue flopped back out again, the fly still stuck to the end, buzzing angrily. Creature pulled the fly off and offered it to his new friend.

"JEE-PURRRRRRRR!"

The new Creature batted the fly away crossly. Suddenly it spotted something interesting over Creature's shoulder. It jumped down from the table and scampered away across the smoky hall.

Creature nearly tripped over his long, froggy tongue as he hurried to follow, clutching his flower close to his hairy chest.

Nora, Jake, and Alexis glanced at each other, then raced after them.

"They're going to wreck the place!" Jake cried as they tried to keep up with the two Creatures. The Creatures were leapfrogging over every table in their way, sending science experiments flying all over the place.

Nora was sprinting and following just behind Jake. "I know they'll cause trouble," she cried, "but how can we catch two? One's bad enough — WATCH OUT!"

Jake skidded to a halt, barely avoiding a gush of steaming liquid from an experiment through which the two Creatures had just steamrollered.

Jake wiped his forehead. *Phew!* That was a close one.

"Now is our chance," Alexis said, pointing.

Ahead, Jake saw Creature catch up with the new Creature and offer it the now rather sad marigold. Jake started to run forward, but Nora grabbed him.

"Awwwww, wait, Jake. That's so sweet."

The new Creature looked at the marigold. Then it stuffed it in its mouth, chewed, and swallowed.

"BUUUURRRRRPPP!"

Then it picked its nose, and pulled out a large, green snot ball. The Creature shyly offered it to Creature.

Creature squeaked happily. He reached out and grabbed the snot ball, flattened it out, and carefully stuck it to his chest, like a badge of honor.

"Ugh!" Nora said, making a face. "That's *not* so sweet!"

The new Creature poked Creature playfully, jumped to its feet, and bounded off into the smoke cloud. It seemed to be heading toward the huge volcano in the center of the hall.

Creature raced after it in a hurry, with Jake, Nora, and Alexis on his furry heels. Jake noticed that Creature's froggy legs had disappeared and he was back to his normal, furry self.

As they rounded the volcano, Alexis
stopped, and her face went a sickly shade of
frog green.

"Oh my!" she gasped. "I don't like the look
of this at ALL."

CHAPTER 6:

SPIDERS AREN'T SCARY

"What is it?"

Jake peered around the volcano, trying to see what had spooked Alexis.

A few feet away, the two Creatures were crouching in front of a table stacked with glass tanks.

A sign read: *SPIDERS AREN'T SCARY*.

"Fab — spiders!" Nora said, stepping forward. Alexis yanked her back.

"No *way* am I going near those things!"

"You shouldn't be scared of spiders, Alexis," Nora said upset.

"I'm not scared." Alexis took a deep breath. "I'm, um, allergic to spiders."

Jake recognized the biggest tank. Taking a look inside, he could see the huge spider he'd narrowly avoided petting in the lobby.

Nora peered at it. "Looks like a tarantula."

"It's a Goliath bird-eating spider," Jake said.

Alexis groaned and closed her eyes.

Nora looked impressed. "How —" She stopped, her eyes widening. "Oh no!"

"What's happening?" Alexis squeaked.

Creature had jumped up next to the tank, squashed his face to the glass, and was making faces at the huge, hairy spider. The spider glared back at him through eight glittering, black eyes.

Creature chuckled. He glanced down at the new Creature, as if to say, "Aren't I funny?"

The new Creature squawked back, as if to say, "No, you are certainly not funny."

Jake shook his head. "He'll make the spider angry. We've got to stop him."

"You grab him, I'll grab the new Creature," Nora said grimly.

"Eeeeek!" The new Creature suddenly gave a high-pitched squeak. Creature was pulling the lid of the tank off! He put a paw in and fished the spider out of the tank.

"STOP!" Jake dashed forward.

Creature spun around, the spider crouching on his paw.

"Eeeeeeeee?" Creature said. He held the spider up to his lips . . .

"DON'T EAT IT!" shrieked Nora.

. . . And gave it a big kiss.

The spider looked at Creature with all eight eyes. Then it bit him on the nose.

"Jeep-PEEEEERRRRRRRR!"

Creature dropped the spider into its tank and jumped upward, disappearing into the cloud of smoke still on the ceiling.

Jake ran forward, arms outstretched to catch him . . .

But Creature didn't fall back down. Confused, Jake peered up. *Where was he?* Then, through a gap in the smoke, he saw a brown, hairy shape on the ceiling.

It had Creature's head. But it also had an enormous, balloon-like bottom, and eight extremely hairy legs.

"He's turned into a *spider*!" Nora gasped.

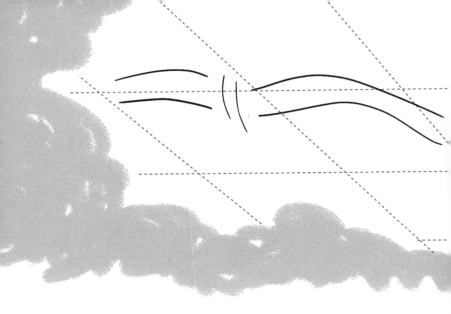

Alexis opened her eyes a crack, screamed, and closed them again. Jake felt the hairs on the back of his neck rise. Then he remembered the new Creature.

"Where'd the other one go?"

They all looked around. The new Creature was nowhere to be seen.

Nora bit her lip. "What should we do?"

Jake looked up at Spider-Creature on the ceiling. "We'll have to try to catch Creature

first, then look for the new one. Oh no,
where's he going now?"

Spider-Creature was skittering along
the ceiling. Jake and Nora ran after him,
followed reluctantly by Alexis.

"Why do you think he keeps changing?"
Jake called to Nora as they dodged tables,
trying to keep Creature in sight.

"It's a guess, but maybe the electric shock
jumbled his cells up."

"And what does that mean?" asked Jake.

"It means that maybe now he can change into anything, with the right catalyst."

"What's a catalyst?" Jake asked.

"A catalyst is a chemical that sets off a reaction. You can think of it sort of like a trigger —"

"GET DOWN!" Alexis suddenly called.

Jake looked around. "What?"

"Rule-Bot!"

Class 5A's robot was rolling toward them. Jake, Nora, and Alexis dived behind a stand. *Had he seen them?*

Jake peered out cautiously. Rule-Bot had stopped in front of the Make Sparks Fly stand.

Nora tutted. "Barnaby's supposed to be keeping Rule-Bot busy! Where's he gone?"

"*Everyone's* gone," said Alexis.

Jake looked around. Now the smoke was clearing, he could see that the hall was nearly empty of people.

At the far wall, a museum worker was using an oversized rug to waft smoke out of a nearby window.

"They'll be back once the smoke's cleared," Jake said. "Then there'll be trouble."

"Squarrrk!"

A startled squawk came from above. Jake looked up.

Creature's round spider bottom was shrinking, and his fur was changing back to red-brown. One by one, his spider legs were disappearing. As they did so, Creature was coming unstuck from the ceiling!

Jake held his breath. *He's turning back into normal Creature — and I'm too far away to catch him!*

Creature was now hanging on with one last spider leg. As it changed back into a normal paw, it lost its grip on the ceiling, and Creature fell into space.

"Nooooooo!" Nora cried, clutching Jake's arm so hard he yelped.

But Creature clearly still had a bit of spider in him. No sooner had he fallen than a strand of silver thread fired out of his bottom like a grappling hook. It hit the ceiling and stuck on tight.

Creature began to float gently down on his silver rope.

Jake breathed out. "*Phew* . . . OW!" Nora had clutched his arm again.

"You know where he's going to land, don't you?" she asked urgently.

Jake's eyes widened. "Oh no! He's going to land on Rule-Bot's head!"

Rule-Bot was still in front of the
Make Sparks Fly stand, staring at
the Van de Graaff generator.
A large, flashing love heart
appeared on his screen.

He beeped softly.

Jake, Nora, and Alexis
stared, open-mouthed, as
Creature floated

down . . .

down . . .

down . . .

. . . till he was hanging just over the unsuspecting Rule-Bot's head.

Creature blew a loud raspberry.

The love heart on Rule-Bot's screen vanished, to be replaced with a very sad face. His head whizzed around. But although his head could swivel in a full circle, he couldn't look up. So he couldn't see Creature at all.

Creature blew another, louder raspberry.

Rule-Bot spun around so fast he nearly fell over. Alexis giggled, but Jake ran forward.

"Hey, Rule-Bot! Over here!" he shouted at the confused robot.

Too late.

SNAP! The silver thread broke.

Creature dropped — *CLUNK!* — straight onto Rule-Bot's head.

CHAPTER 7:

ANT ANTICS

For two seconds, nothing happened.

Then everything happened. All at once. Very fast.

"BEEEEEEEPPP!" Rule-Bot's head whizzed round and round, his blue light flashing madly.

"Wheeeeeeeeeeeee!" Creature clung on for dear life, legs flying out behind him. On the third spin, he lost his grip, catapulted through the air, and landed on the Make Sparks Fly table, luckily just missing the Van de Graaff generator.

Rule-Bot charged after him, his claw-like hands outstretched . . .

Creature stepped to one side.

CLANG! Rule-Bot's metal hand slammed into the Van de Graaff generator.

CRAAAAAAAAAACK!

A burst of blue sparks exploded from Rule-Bot's head.

"VIOLATION OF RULE SEVEN THOUSAND THREE HUNDRED AND TWO — NEVER JUMP ON RULE-BOT'S HEAD!" the robot rasped.

Nora stared. "There's no such rule!"

Rule-Bot turned to face Nora.

"VIOLATION OF RULE EIGHT MILLION AND SEVENTY THREE — DO NOT CONTRADICT RULE-BOT!"

Jake, Nora, and Alexis dove out of the way as a stream of stickers flew out of Rule-Bot's tummy slot. People were filing back into the hall now, and a crowd started to gather around the sparking, spinning robot.

"STAND BACK! Let me deal with this . . ."

A red-faced Mrs. Blunt was bulldozing her way through the crowd. She pointed a remote control at Rule-Bot.

CRACKLE . . . SIZZLE . . . WHOOSH!

A shower of multicolored sparks exploded from Rule-Bot's head.

"VIOLATION OF RULE TWO BILLION AND ONE! MA'AM, YOU ARE UNDER ARREST!" shouted Rule-Bot at Mrs. Blunt.

"You can't arrest me, you dim-witted robot," Mrs. Blunt snapped. She crouched down and pointed the remote at Rule-Bot's tummy slot.

"Mmmmmmffff!"

A stream of stickers flew out, covering the principal's surprised face. She let out a muffled shriek and tried to peel them off, but they just kept on coming until she could barely be seen under a thick layer of Sad Faces. A few people rushed forward to try and help, but they just got stickered themselves. It was a very stickery situation.

"Jeepperrrrrrrrrrr . . ."

Jake dragged his eyes away from the chaos to see Creature perching on the end of the Make Sparks Fly table, gazing across at the Ant Antics stand.

Jake tensed and inched forward.

Slowly . . . don't scare him . . .

Jake sprang . . .

. . . but his elbows hit the table where Creature had been a second before. As he scrambled up, he saw Creature bouncing toward the Ant Antics stand.

"After him!" Jake shouted to Nora and Alexis.

Leaving the sticker battle behind, they pushed through the crowd after Creature.

Jake saw Creature reach the stand and hop up onto the edge of the formicarium, where he perched, swaying, and peered around.

I bet he's looking for that new Creature, Jake guessed. He looked around, but didn't see it anywhere. Luckily, neither Isaac nor Miss Jex were anywhere to be seen, either.

"GOTCHA!"

Alexis hurled herself past Jake, toward Creature. Alarmed, Creature turned, wobbled, then tumbled into the formicarium in an explosion of dirt and ants.

Jake, Nora, and Alexis ran forward to try to grab him. But as they closed in, he leapt back up and began dancing around like a loon, slapping himself all over.

"The ants are biting him!" Nora exclaimed.

Biting? Alarm bells jangled in Jake's head as he remembered Nora's earlier words: *Creature can change into anything given the right catalyst.*

"STAY BACK!" he cried.

Jake reached out and pulled Alexis and Nora backward — just as two antennae grew out of Creature's head, his eyes went all buggy, and a pair of humongous mandibles sprouted from his chin.

CLICK! CLACK! Ant-Creature snapped his new, shiny mandibles.

At the same time, Jake heard a familiar electronic rasp.

"ANT INVASION DETECTED! ANTI-ANT PROGRAM ACTIVATED! EX-TERM-IN-ATE! EX-TERM-IN-ATE!"

Rule-Bot!

Creature's buggy eyes nearly popped out as Rule-Bot charged toward the table at top speed. Jake ran forward to stop him, but Rule-Bot turned at the last minute — too sharply! He spun out of control, straight into one of the table legs.

CRACK!

The leg snapped. Nora gave a cry. "The table!" she shouted. "It's falling over!"

They all dove forward and grabbed the edge of the table as it started to teeter . . . but the huge formicarium was too heavy.

"Can't . . . hold . . . it," Jake panted, as the formicarium, ten thousand ants, and one Creature slid with a horrible grinding noise toward the edge . . .

C-R-A-SHHHH!

The tank smashed into a thousand tiny pieces on the floor.

The three kids gaped in alarmed silence.

Nora put her hands to her mouth. "Isaac will be so upset!"

A carpet of angry ants began to spread out from the huge mess. Creature sat dazed in the middle of it as Rule-Bot wheeled around to face him, siren wailing.

"EX-TERM-IN-ATE!

EX-TERM-IN-ATE!"

Jake tried to dart in front of the robot, but had to jump back to avoid a blast of bright, blue sparks.

"HEY! What's going on?"

Karl skidded up, Woodstock and Barnaby behind him.

"Rule-Bot's trying to exterminate Creature," said Jake. "We have to stop him!"

The six students fanned out around Rule-Bot, now covered in ants. He screeched to a halt, trying to sweep them off with his mechanical hand.

"ALL ANTS ARE UNDER ARREST!"

The ants kept crawling. Rule-Bot got more and more annoyed. He swiveled his head toward Creature.

"BAD KING ANT. MAKE SMALL ANTS ATTACK RULE-BOT. EX-TERM-IN-ATE!"

"I can see the off-switch!" shouted Nora, suddenly. "Distract him!"

Alexis, Karl, and Woodstock dashed in, yelling and waving. But Rule-Bot kept rolling toward Creature, metal arms outstretched menacingly. Jake could see that Creature's antennae and mandibles were shrinking. He was changing back into normal Creature, and he looked completely terrified.

"It's not working!" Nora cried. "Barnaby, you try!"

Barnaby ran to one side and started blowing raspberries.

"You're nothing but a ratty old toaster!" he shouted.

Jake got the idea.

"Work together, everyone! Over here, you worn-out wastebasket!" he yelled.

"Lazy lawnmower!"

"Horrid Hoover!"

Rule-Bot's head swung around to face the yelling students. As soon as his head was turned, Nora took her chance. She dove under his arm.

"Got it!" She pushed a button.

There was a crackle and then a hum.

"Bedtime," Rule-Bot said in a sad, tinny voice.

His screen flickered, and went black.

CHAPTER 8:

VOLCANIC CHATTER

Everyone ran to the quivering Creature. Jake looked around anxiously. *Had anyone seen what had happened?* Jake wondered. He figured it wasn't likely since people were only just starting to come back into the hall. Besides, most of them were busy trying to clear up the mess caused by all the explosions earlier.

"He's covered in ants!" exclaimed Alexis, crouching down and brushing ants off of Creature's nose.

"Poor thing! Are you okay?" Nora asked.

Creature stared at her and squeaked softly. Then he closed his eyes. Jake heard a faint humming.

"Hmmmmmmmmmmm . . ."

Woodstock nudged Jake. "Look!"

Jake stared. A faint, wobbly heat haze surrounded Creature. There was a loud rumble.

"Jeepperrrrrrr?" Creature looked at his tummy.

"He's changing back into Mr. Hyde! We have to get him back to our stand," said Nora.

She whisked Creature up and stuffed him under her lab coat. Jake and the others formed a protective huddle around her as they hurried back to The Nose.

A series of violent rumbles made the floor vibrate under their feet.

"Where can we put him?" Nora cried.

Jake looked around. "In The Nose!"

They pushed Creature inside, and stood back. Jake covered his eyes, waiting for the fireworks. The rumbling got louder and louder. Jake waited expectantly for the usual signs of the change — bright lights . . . fart . . . pop! pop! pop!

But something was different. The rumbling didn't seem to be coming from Creature! So where was it coming from? Jake took his hands away from his eyes.

The hall was packed with people again. But all the people were standing as still as statues, all facing the same way, all staring. Staring at . . .

The volcano exhibit! Jake grabbed Nora.

"It's not *Creature* that's rumbling!" he shouted. "It's the volcano!"

All six students wheeled around. As they did so, the volcano let out a piercing squeal.

Wheeeeeeeeeeeeeeeeeee . . . .

"I think something's stuck inside it," Nora exclaimed.

WHEEEEEEEEEEEEEEEE . . .

The squeal got louder and louder. Everyone in the room covered their ears . . .

POP!

With a sound like a huge champagne cork popping, a large, oddly-shaped lump of rock shot out of the top of the volcano, trailing a sticky red lava trail behind it. It whizzed across the hall, right over Jake's head. As it sailed over, he heard it making a particularly unrocklike noise.

"JEEPPPPPPPPPPURRRRRRRRRRRRRRRR!" it shrieked, arm stretched out in front of it like a superhero. Unlike a superhero, it landed with a painful-looking thump and rolled through a door at the back of the hall.

Nora was beside Jake like a shot.

"That was the new Creature!" she cried.

"What new Creature?" a familiar voice said behind them.

Jake turned. "MR. HYDE!"

Mr. Hyde was standing where The Nose had been. He was covered in the mangled remains of The Nose and had purple snot dripping down his face, but apart from that he looked normal. Jake had been so busy watching the volcano erupt that he hadn't even noticed Creature changing back into Mr. Hyde!

Mr. Hyde looked down at himself.

"Why am I wearing a papier-mâché dress?"

"It's The Nose, sir. We hid you in it when you started changing," Jake said. "I forgot you'd get bigger when you changed back."

Everyone ran to help free their teacher. As he stepped out of the last tattered remains of The Nose, Mr. Hyde looked at Nora.

"What was that you were saying about a new Creature?"

"Yes, what do you mean, Nora?" Karl asked. Barnaby and Woodstock leaned in, curious.

"Well, there was another Creature that looked just like you," Nora explained.

"But it disappeared when you changed into a spider." Jake added.

"A spider?" Woodstock interrupted. "Mr. Hyde turned into a spider?"

"Yes — that was a little while after he changed into a frog."

"A frog?" Karl looked disbelieving.

"It's true! And before he turned into—"

"An ant." Mr. Hyde finished his sentence.

Jake blinked. "You remember?"

"I remember parts," Mr. Hyde said slowly. "Like you remember a dream. I remember eating a jar of weird-tasting jelly . . . and then wanting to hop around. And I remember the spider biting me on the nose, and next thing I was running around on the ceiling . . ."

"I didn't like it when you were a spider." Alexis said.

"I quite enjoyed it," said Mr. Hyde. "I didn't like being an ant, though. That yelling robot scared me. But I remember all of you kids protecting me, and that gave me a warm, nice feeling."

"Don't you remember the new Creature?" Nora asked.

Mr. Hyde shook his head. "Not at all. Are you sure? How on earth could there be another Creature?"

"We think —" Nora took a deep breath. "In fact, we're pretty sure — that you have been cloned."

Mr. Hyde stared. "Cloned?"

Jake explained. "One of the exhibits is a cloning experiment. We think you must have somehow got into it, and cloned yourself."

"Only it didn't quite work," Nora added. "The new Creature has different hair from you."

Karl's eyes widened. "Oh man. Clone Creature. Double trouble!"

Barnaby's eyes went misty. "Wish *I* had a clone!"

"I don't know," Mr. Hyde said. "I think I'd remember being cloned . . ."

"But you don't remember the new Creature, either," Jake broke in. "That's definitely real — *and* it's running around somewhere in the next hall," he reminded Nora. "We have to go and find it!"

Mr. Hyde suddenly shot bolt upright.

"Yes, we should — RIGHT NOW!"

Jake looked at his teacher's panic-stricken face. "What's the matter, sir?" he asked.

Mr. Hyde gulped.

"If it is a clone of Creature, will it change back into a clone of *me*?"

Jake's mouth fell open. But before he could say anything, there was a shout.

"HEY! Nora Newton! I need to talk to you!"

A wild-eyed Isaac was streaking across the hall toward them.

CHAPTER 9:

A BIT OF AN EYE-OPENER

Nora gulped. "Isaac! He must have seen the formicarium . . ."

Isaac skidded to a halt in front of them.

"What's the matter, Isaac?" Mr. Hyde asked.

"I have to show you something," he whispered, glancing around secretively. Jake gave Nora an anxious glance. Mr. Hyde's brow creased.

"It's a bit difficult—"

"Oh please, you must!" Isaac begged.

Mr. Hyde relented. "Weeeell . . . OK. But we'll have to be quick."

Isaac nodded. "Follow me!"

Jake thought Isaac would take them to his stand. But instead, he led them to the back of the hall and out through the same door the new Creature had disappeared through. They emerged into another hall, full of telescopes and globes.

"Keep your eyes peeled," Jake whispered to the others. "The new Creature came this way!"

"Over here," Isaac called. He was standing in front of a door with a sign on it that read *EMERGENCY USE ONLY*.

Mr. Hyde frowned. "Isaac, I don't think—"

"This *is* an emergency," Isaac said. "You'll understand in a minute."

He pushed the door open and stepped inside.

"Oh dear . . ." Mr. Hyde hesitated, then followed Isaac. Jake and the others crowded in behind them.

EMERGENCY
USE ONLY

Once Jake's eyes adjusted to the dark, he could see huge shapes draped in white sheets. *A storage room*, Jake thought.

"We shouldn't be in here," Mr. Hyde said. His voice boomed back.

"HERE . . . here . . . here . . ."

Barnaby burped. "*BURP . . . burp . . . burp . . .*"

"Shh!" Isaac said. "You'll scare it."

"Scare what?" Karl asked.

Isaac walked across the nearest sheet and carefully lifted the corner.

"Look," he whispered.

Jake peered underneath — then jolted back! He was looking straight into the tooth-lined jaws of a monster! Then he realized what it was.

"It's just a dinosaur skull," he said. But wait — *what was that?* Two pinpricks of

light. *They were eyes!* Little, bright eyes, moving toward him . . . and they belonged to the head of a brown, furry shape . . .

"**Jeeppurrrr?**" it said.

Jake stared, speechless. *The new Creature!* It hopped up onto the dinosaur's lower jawbone and peered curiously at Isaac.

"It's . . ." Nora's voice trailed off.

Isaac looked at her. "Do you know something about this?"

Nora gulped. Mr. Hyde spoke. "Nora, let me explain. That Creature is . . . well, I'm afraid it's *me*."

"What?" Isaac gasped.

"It's true," Mr. Hyde said. "I change into a Creature just like this."

Everyone started talking at once.

"And today, while he was Creature—"

"— he somehow got cloned!"

"And now there are two—"

"Stop! Listen . . ." Isaac shook his head.
The new Creature shook its head too. As it
did so, something jingled in its hair.

Nora pointed. "Look! Miss Jex's earrings!"

Dangling from each of the Creature's ears Jake saw the Saturn-shaped earrings Miss Jex had been wearing earlier.

Barnaby grinned. "It must have stolen them!"

Nora rolled her eyes. "She'll be so mad!"

"LET ME SPEAK!" Isaac shouted.

Everyone stopped talking.

"The Creature isn't Mr. Hyde," Isaac said. "And it didn't steal Miss Jex's earrings."

Nora looked puzzled. "So who . . ."

Isaac cleared his throat. "The Creature IS Miss Jex!"

There was an astonished silence.

"Miss Jex?" Mr. Hyde's mouth fell open.

Isaac nodded. "I couldn't find Miss Jex earlier, so I went back to our stand. I found this Creature hiding under Miss Jex's coat. I thought it had escaped from another stand.

It ran off, and I lost it in all the smoke and chaos. I went around the whole museum looking for Miss Jex. As I was coming back through the astronomy hall I saw this Creature run into this storage room, so I followed it. When I finally caught it, I realized that it *was* Miss Jex!"

"How do you know for sure?" Mr. Hyde asked, looking pained.

"The red hair and glasses were the first clue. And the earrings almost convinced me. But I'm a scientist — I need proof. Glasses and earrings don't *prove* anything . . ." Isaac picked up the wide-eyed little Creature. "But EYES do."

Jake stared at the Creature. It stared back. There was something odd about its eyes . . . then he noticed what it was. One was sapphire blue, the other emerald green!

Nora gasped. "Miss Jex has different-colored eyes."

Isaac turned to Nora. "I thought I was going crazy! Then I thought of you, Nora. I thought you might have an idea about how this happened."

Nora stared. "Me? But I thought you thought my ideas were *silly!*"

Isaac looked surprised. "I don't think that," he said. "You're smart — the smartest person I know."

Nora flushed. "Oh, um, thanks," she mumbled, embarrassed.

A door banged on the other side of the storage room, making everyone jump.

"Someone's coming," Woodstock hissed.

"Eep!" Miss Jex muttered in fright.

"Time to go!" shouted Jake.

"Here . . ." Mr. Hyde grabbed Miss Jex from Isaac, stuffed her under his coat, and ran to the door. "Hurry!"

One by one they ran through, back into the astronomy hall.

Mr. Hyde looked around. "We have to get Miss Jex out of the museum."

"The only way is back through the Science Fair," Isaac said.

They trooped back into the main hall, that now looked more like a major disaster zone than a Science Fair.

As they approached the door to the main entrance, Jake saw Mrs. Blunt standing directly in front of it with a grim look on her face.

"Bad idea. Back to the stand," Mr. Hyde said, turning on his heel.

As they approached the Ant Antics stand, Jake saw a group of sharply dressed people standing in front of it. His mouth suddenly felt like he'd eaten dry crackers and his hands got all clammy. *Is it the Museum Police? Are they looking for Miss Jex? Will they arrest us?*

A loudspeaker crackled.

"Would the Ant Antics and the Have You Got a Tissue teams please return to your stands immediately to present your work to the judges."

CHAPTER 10:

TEN THOUSAND ANTS AND A BUCKET-LOAD OF SNOT

"The judges!" Isaac gulped. "I'd totally forgotten about the competition!"

One judge spotted them.

"Are you the Ant Antics team?" she called, waving a clipboard.

"We have been waiting for you," said another, staring at them over his steel-rimmed spectacles.

"For approximately fifty-three seconds," said another judge, tapping his watch.

Isaac shuffled forward. "It's just m-m-me," he stammered. "My teacher has, um, well, changed . . ."

"Gone to *get* changed," Mr. Hyde said quickly, pulling his coat around the bulge that was Miss Jex. "She got lava from the volcano all over her."

Jake saw that even the judges looked a bit lava-splattered. The judge with the clipboard, who seemed to be the head judge, frowned.

"Most unfortunate, but I'm afraid we can't wait. Please proceed."

Isaac cleared his throat.

"Ahem. Ant Antics is an interesting project about . . . ants. Um . . . we have approximately ten thousand ants —"

"I don't see any ants," a judge interrupted.

"Invisible ants?" said another. "Now that would be a first!"

The judges roared with laughter. The small crowd of onlookers who had gathered to watch the judging laughed too.

Isaac went beet red.

"They're not invisible — they're in the formicari . . ."

He pointed. Everyone looked around.

". . . um . . ." Isaac's voice trailed away. "It's gone!"

He was pointing at a large, empty, ant-free stand.

Jake gulped. *Isaac doesn't know about Rule-Bot smashing the formicarium!*

He obviously hadn't been back to the stand since it happened. Someone must have been around with a broom — there wasn't a trace of glass or dirt anywhere. And not a single ant in sight. Even the broken table was missing.

Should I tell him? Jake decided it wasn't a good moment — Isaac looked like he might burst into tears.

Nora ran up to the head judge, who was scribbling *DISQUALIFIED* on her clipboard.

"Oh please don't disqualify Isaac! His exhibit was really good—"

"I can only judge what I can see," the judge snapped. "All right, moving on. There's still one more exhibit to go."

Nora went quiet. Jake saw that she was shaking. A vision of the tattered remains of The Nose flashed in front of his eyes. There'd been virtually nothing left after they'd got Mr. Hyde out of it! But the judges were already walking toward their stand.

The head judge shuffled her notes. "The next one is . . . *Have You Got a Tissue? Should be* — ah, this is it . . ."

There was a stunned silence.

Aargh. I can't look. Jake fixed his eyes firmly on the floor.

As he looked, he saw something moving. *An ant!* It was carrying something. Almost instinctively, he bent down and picked it up. *The last surviving ant. Isaac might want it . . .* He heard an exclamation from Nora. And a cry from Alexis.

"My word," he heard one of the judges say. "Extraordinary!"

"Breathtaking!" said another.

"Mind-boggling!" said another.

Jake slowly looked up. He rubbed his eyes, then looked again.

Where the Giant Nose had been there now stood a glistening, purple structure. Nearly as tall as Jake himself, it was covered with a network of delicate, semi-transparent spires and bridges. It reminded Jake of the time his parents had taken him to Disneyland and he'd seen the Cinderella castle at night, all lit up with purple lights.

What on earth was it? The last he'd seen of their stand, it had been a chaotic mess of purple snot and . . . but wait a minute.

Jake stared at the structure. Something was moving on it. *Ants! Thousands of them. But what are they doing?* He looked back at the ant that he had picked up.

"Isaac — hold out your hand!" Jake whispered.

Isaac looked surprised but did as Jake asked. Jake carefully placed the ant on Isaac's palm.

"Look at what it's carrying!" he said. Isaac lifted his hand and stared at the ant. Nora leaned in too. They spoke as one.

"Purple snot!"

"Isaac! Your ants have built a new home with our snot!" she exclaimed.

Isaac blinked. "Are you thinking what I'm thinking?"

"I think so . . ." She grinned. "Come on!"

They both ran over to the judges.

"Please . . . Isaac and I would like to introduce our cross-school project," said Nora.

The head judge flipped through her notes. "There's nothing here about cross-school projects!"

"Let them speak," said another judge. "I think we should hear what they've got to say."

"Quiet, please!" called Nora.

Isaac held up the ant that Jake had given him.

"One tiny ant," he said. "Can't do much on its own."

Nora gestured to the ant palace, dramatically. "But as part of a team, it can create architectural miracles!"

"In order to conduct an experiment to learn what ants can do when they work together . . ."

"Isaac released ten thousand ants into the wild . . ."

". . . and using Nora's unique formula of sugar, flour, and water —"

"And purple food dye," Woodstock called.

"And purple food dye . . . these ants built themselves a new colony . . ."

The judges were impressed. Jake was too. It was as though Nora and Isaac had rehearsed their whole speech, when he knew they actually were making it up as they went!

"So we humans can learn a great deal from ants . . ." Isaac said.

". . . by working together, we can achieve anything!" Nora finished.

"HURRAY!"

A roar of applause made Jake jump. He looked around to find himself surrounded by people, all clapping and cheering. Mr. Hyde was wiping his eyes. He saw Jake looking at him and coughed.

"Bit fumy in here," he mumbled.

The judges put their heads together, muttering, as the crowd chattered excitedly. The head judge stepped forward.

"Quiet, please!" she shouted. The hall fell silent. "The judges will now proceed to the stage to announce the official winner of the Whiz-BANG Brainiest Whiz Kid Competition."

CHAPTER 11:

AND THE WINNER IS . . .

The judges marched across the hall. Jake and his friends followed, swept along on a tide of chattering people.

"You were awesome!" Jake said to Nora as they reached the stage.

Nora smiled nervously. "Awesome enough to win?"

"HA! You've got no chance, goggle girl!" a voice called.

Jake winced, and turned to see Amelia Trotter-Hogg and her two clinging friends smirking at him.

"And what makes you think you have a chance, Amelia?" Nora snapped. "Rule-Bot is faulty. He went completely loopy."

Amelia shrugged. "We fixed him."

A flash of anger surged through Jake. "You mean the *Professor* fixed him?"

"Prove it," Amelia spat.

"SILENCE, PLEASE!" called the head judge.

Jake could have heard an ant burp in the silence.

"We are pleased to announce . . ."

She paused. Jake's heart leapt.

". . . that the winning exhibit is . . ."

Oh please . . . it has to be us . . .

"Rule-Bot — the rule-enforcing robot!"

WHAT? Jake could hardly believe his ears. He couldn't bring himself to look at Nora as Amelia and her friends skipped past them onto the stage, evil glee on their faces.

"MAKE WAY! Winner coming through!" Mrs. Blunt swept up the steps onto the stage, where she stood waving importantly at the crowd. There was a splatter of polite clapping.

The head judge handed Amelia a microphone. "Would you like to say a few words?"

Mrs. Blunt grabbed the microphone.

"Yes, I would, thank you. It is a great honor for me — I mean *us* — to receive this award. The Prof . . . er . . . *these proud students* put a lot of hard work into Rule-Bot. Its discipline circuits are second to none — all designed by the students, of course."

"VIOLATION OF RULE 999! DO NOT TELL STINKY LIES!" said a tinny voice.

Mrs. Blunt glared around. "Who said that?"

Jake looked around to see a flashing blue light moving jerkily through the crowd.

Rule-Bot! The robot stopped in front of the stage. Amelia and her friends shuffled back uneasily.

"LIE DETECTOR ACTIVATED! STUDENTS NOT DESIGN RULE-BOT! PROFESSOR QUARK DESIGN RULE-BOT!"

A murmur rippled around the audience.

"Is this true?" the head judge asked sternly. "The rules state that students must design their own exhibits!"

"Of course it's not true!" Mrs. Blunt smiled through gritted teeth.

"So who is Professor Quark?" said another judge.

"PROFESSOR QUARK DESIGN ROBOTS!" rasped Rule-Bot.

Jake saw a man's face appear on Rule-Bot's screen, with a smile as dazzling as one on a toothpaste advertisement.

"Greetings! I am Professor Ignominious Quark. Need a robot? Not got the skills? Better call Quark!" the man oozed, smiling with all his teeth.

"Oooooooooh!" murmured the crowd.

Mrs. Blunt's smile leapt off her face.

"YOU ARE A CHEATER!" Rule-Bot barked.

"And *you* are a tiny, tin-brained traitor!" Mrs. Blunt raged, frantically fumbling in her bag. She pulled out her remote control, pointed it at the robot, and pressed a button.

ZWAP!

Rule-Bot went quiet.

"That's how you deal with a badly-behaved robot!" Mrs. Blunt said, triumphantly. "If only one could do the same for ch—"

Her voice faltered.

Every light on Rule-Bot's metal body lit up.

His head began to spin around, faster and faster, shooting out multicolored sparks like a firework and squealing like a Roman candle.

"SQUEEEEEEEEEEEEEEE ..."

"It's going to blow!" someone shouted.

Rule-Bot didn't explode.

A sheet of electric blue flame burst from his head and flowed down him like glowing water.

"ALERT! ALERT!" Rule-Bot slurred. "OVERHEATING! OVEEEEEEEERRRRRR HEEEEATINGGGGGGGGGGG AAAAARGHHH."

With a final tragic sigh, Rule-Bot collapsed into a puddle of melted metal.

Jake stood, stunned, as the crowd surged forward to gape at the steaming pool of liquefied robot. The judges looked helplessly out at the chaos.

"Explosions, eruptions, melting robots!" one said. "What next? The end of the universe?"

"Look over there, I've never seen Amelia and Mrs. Blunt move so fast!" Karl laughed.

Jake looked across the stage to see Amelia and Mrs. Blunt running down the steps, looking as though they wanted to melt into the floor too.

"We should stop them," Alexis exclaimed, ready to spring off after them. "They can't just get away with cheating."

Jake grabbed her. "Leave it. They won't win now, anyway."

"Who will, though?" Nora said.

Woodstock pointed. "Looks like we're about to find out."

The judges were walking to the front of the stage. The head judge clapped her hands.

"Please listen, everyone. This has been a difficult day, to say the least. However, we have chosen a new winner."

Jake held his breath.

The judge cleared her throat. "We are happy to announce that the winner of the Whiz-BANG Brainiest Whiz Kid Competition is . . . the *Ant Palace*!"

"HURRAY!" The crowd whooped gleefully.

"Yay!" Jake high-fived Nora. Isaac tried to high-five Jake. He missed and whacked Alexis on the ear instead, but she was too busy gleefully punching Barnaby on the arm to notice.

"Excuse me, when you have finished bashing each other, could two of you come up here to collect the medals?" the judge called down to them severely, but Jake thought he saw a twinkle in her eye.

Nora and Isaac bounded onto the stage. The judge hung a gold medal around each of their necks and shook their hands.

"Well done!" she shouted over deafening cheers. Nora and Isaac looked at each other, beaming with pride. Jake thought his face would split from grinning . . . but then he heard a yelp behind him.

"Jake!" Mr. Hyde hissed.

Jake turned. "Sir?"

Mr. Hyde's coat was bulging out as if he had a gang of overenthusiastic moles under it. *Miss Jex!* Alarmed, Jake stepped forward.

PAAAAAAAAAARP!

Mr. Hyde's coat inflated like a hot air balloon.

Ping! Ping! Ping!

Miss Jex burst out of the coat with a button-busting fart. Jake tried to grab her, but she was too quick for him. With a victorious squawk, she skittered off into the crowd.

CHAPTER 12:

THE FATHER OF EVOLUTION

Jake heard startled shrieks from the crowd as Miss Jex darted between their legs.

"MISS JEX!" cried Mr. Hyde, charging after her. Jake, Woodstock, Alexis, and Barnaby tried desperately to keep up.

"Excuse me . . . escaped giant chinchilla . . . perfectly harmless . . . no need to panic . . ."

The crowd panicked.

"WHAT did he say it was?"

"A gorilla?"

"Gorilla on the loose!"

"CALL THE POLICE!"

As he burst out of the crowd, Jake saw a little brown shape shoot through the door to the museum lobby, with Mr. Hyde close behind. As he reached the door, Mr. Hyde slammed to a halt and threw himself back against the wall.

Jake caught up. "What's wrong, sir?" He peered into the lobby.

Mrs. Blunt and Amelia were standing at the reception desk, talking angrily to the man behind it. Behind them, Miss Jex was skipping across the floor toward the museum's huge revolving doors.

Jake held his breath. They hadn't seen her. She was going to make it!

"JEEPPPPPPPPPPPPPPURRRRRRRR!"

Miss Jex made an impressive leap into the revolving doors.

"What the —?" The man at the desk shot up from his seat.

"A GIANT RAT!" shrieked Amelia, hurling herself onto the desk.

Mrs. Blunt's eyes narrowed. "Rats don't say 'Jeeper'!" she snarled.

She stomped her way to the doors. Inside, Miss Jex was running round and round like a crazy hamster in a wheel.

"I've got you now!" shouted Mrs. Blunt.

As the doors swung around, she stepped inside and gave them a shove.

Miss Jex shot out the other side, landing in the museum's courtyard.

Creeaaaaaaaaaaaak . . .
Judder judder judder . . .

CLUNK. The doors stopped. And Mrs. Blunt was inside.

She pushed. She pulled. She pounded.

The revolving doors didn't budge. They were broken.

"LET ME OUT!" she bawled.

"Everyone keep calm!" the man at the desk hollered at the onlookers. Amelia was still babbling about giant rats. Jake stepped back, just as Nora and Isaac came running up.

"What's happening?" Nora panted. "We saw you run off!"

Mr. Hyde and Jake hurriedly explained.

"What do we do, sir?" Karl asked, as people piled past them into the overcrowded lobby.

Mr. Hyde frowned. "Miss Jex could be in danger. We have to go after her."

"How?" asked Nora. "We can't go out."

Barnaby pointed. "Use another door."

In the corner, almost hidden behind a potted plant, Jake saw a fire exit sign.

"Well spotted," said Mr. Hyde. They ran over. Mr. Hyde pushed the bar on the door down and it swung open.

Jake stepped through and found himself in the front courtyard of the museum.

A path led to the front gate and a busy road. By the gate Jake saw a statue of a stern-looking man with a full beard . . . and a strangely-shaped, furry hat . . .

"Miss Jex is on the statue's head!" Alexis called quietly.

"Go slowly — no sudden noises," whispered Mr. Hyde. They tiptoed down the path.

Alexis reached the statue first and started to climb up it. Mr. Hyde spotted Alexis, ready to catch her if she fell. Jake held his breath as she got closer and closer to Miss Jex. She reached out her hand.

"HEY, YOU!"

Everyone froze. A museum worker was running toward them.

"You can't climb on Darwin! He's the Father of Evolution!"

Miss Jex hurled herself off the Father of Evolution and bounced out of the gates. At that moment, Jake saw a moving flash of red through the railings.

"BUS!" he yelled, and took off at a sprint.

Too late! Miss Jex bounced into the road.

SCREEEEEEECH!

The bus skidded to a standstill as Jake teetered on the curb. The others ran up beside him. Nora gave a cry.

"Was she hit?"

"I can't see her!"

Woodstock pointed. "She made it!"

On the other side of the road, a brown furry shape was hopping over a wall, chirping and tooting as it went.

"*Phew!*" Mr. Hyde wiped his forehead. A loud beep from the bus startled him into action. He walked into the road and held his hand up.

"Over you go, kids," he said loudly.

Jake shuffled across, trying not to look at the bus driver who was shouting something that did not sound like, "Have a nice day."

They had barely crossed the road when he screeched off with an angry honk. Mr. Hyde shook his head and gave a tut.

"Some people! All right, folks, we've got a teacher — I mean, Creature — to catch!" called Mr. Hyde to the kids.

He vaulted over the wall. Jake and the others followed.

They found themselves in a pretty, tree-lined park, with picnicking families dotted around. It was a peaceful scene.

"EEEEEEEEEEK!"

Jake saw the people at the closest picnic scatter as Miss Jex bounced onto their picnic blanket, picked up a large cake, and ate it up in one chomp.

"BURRRRRRRRP!"

She bounced off toward the next picnic in a shower of crumbs.

"STOP!" Mr. Hyde sprinted after her.

"Sorry!" Nora shouted to the stunned picnickers, as they sprinted past. Miss Jex swerved off, and disappeared into a clump of trees.

"Spread out," Mr. Hyde puffed. "We can corner her here . . ."

He dived into the bushes, followed by Barnaby, Alexis, and Karl. Isaac and Nora ran one way. Jake and Woodstock ran the other way.

"There!" Jake spotted a path leading into the trees. They dashed down it into a pretty clearing. Jake looked around for Miss Jex.

"She's gone," Woodstock said, frustrated.

Leaves drifted down from a tree nearby. Shading his eyes, Jake squinted up.

"Up there!" He could just see the brown shape of Miss Jex climbing up the trunk.

There was a rustle as Nora and Isaac emerged from a bush.

"Where is she?" cried Isaac. Jake pointed up the tree. Everyone stared up at Miss Jex, leaping from branch to branch.

"She's going to the top," Woodstock said.

Nora clutched her head. "The branches will be too thin!"

Miss Jex swung onto a very thin branch.

SNAP!

The branch broke.

CHAPTER 13:

SQUIRREL POWER

"NOOOOOOOOO!" Nora screamed.

Miss Jex plummeted toward the ground through the upper branches, grabbing desperately — but they were too thin, and snapped instantly. Jake ran forward, arms outstretched.

He caught an armful of leaves and twigs, but no Miss Jex. He looked up.

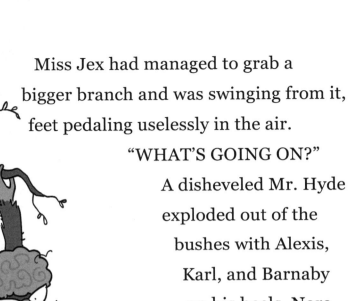

Miss Jex had managed to grab a
bigger branch and was swinging from it,
feet pedaling uselessly in the air.

"WHAT'S GOING ON?"

A disheveled Mr. Hyde
exploded out of the
bushes with Alexis,
Karl, and Barnaby
on his heels. Nora,
Isaac, Jake, and
Woodstock ran
over to him.

"Miss Jex —"

"— up that tree —"

"— she's going to fall!"

Mr. Hyde ran to the tree.
He grabbed a low branch.

"You can do this, Hydey," Jake heard him
mutter to himself.

He swung up onto one branch, then another, reciting a sort of mantra.

"Only a little tree, nothing to be scared of."

Nora clutched Jake's sleeve. "He's scared of heights, remember?" she whispered.

"Don't look down, sir!" Barnaby shouted.

"Nothing to be . . . what?" Mr. Hyde looked down.

His face went a sickly green. He grabbed the trunk and clung to it, shaking.

"Nice one, Barnaby," Jake said, upset.

Alexis ran to the tree. "Let me try, sir," she called.

But Mr. Hyde took a deep breath, then an even bigger gulp, and inched his arm up to another branch.

"Oh, he'll never get there," Isaac groaned, as Mr. Hyde stopped again.

"Eeeeeeek!"

A terrified squawk from Miss Jex made everyone look up. Way up above Mr. Hyde, the branch she was hanging from was beginning to bend.

Clinging to the trunk, Mr. Hyde looked up too. When he saw Miss Jex, his face took on a look of strong determination.

"HANG IN THERE, MISS JEX, I'M COMING FOR YOU!" he bellowed.

With a grunt, he pulled himself up, and began scrambling up the tree.

Jake watched, mouth open, as his teacher shimmied up the trunk like an overgrown squirrel. In less than thirty seconds, he had squirreled up to the branch Miss Jex was hanging from. He began to creep along it toward Miss Jex.

Jake held his breath.

Nora shut her eyes. "I can't look . . ."

The branch, not used to such enormous squirrels, bent further and further over . . .

There was a frightened squawk. One of Miss Jex's paws had slipped off the branch and she was swinging wildly, trying to catch hold of it again.

Mr. Hyde leaned over and made a grab at Miss Jex's flailing paw.

Creeeee- e- e- e- e- ak · · ·

There was a nasty splintering noise.

CRA- A- ACK!

"Aaaaa-ah-ah-ah-aaaaaaah!"

With a Tarzan war cry, Mr. Hyde flung
himself off the branch, scooped Miss Jex up
in his arms, and crashed through leaves to
land on a thick branch a few feet below.

Jake breathed out.

"HE SAVED HER!" Nora grabbed a
startled Isaac and swung him around,
whooping, as Mr. Hyde swung down to the
ground with Miss Jex clinging to him like a
baby monkey.

"Mr. Hyde, you're a hero!" Woodstock
cried.

"Superhero!" Karl added.

"Super-mega-hero!" Nora said proudly.

"How did you do it, sir?" Jake asked. "I mean — you're scared of heights!"

Mr. Hyde looked up at the tree, then at the little Creature in his arms, who was looking up at him with big, sweet eyes.

"I'm not entirely sure," he said thoughtfully.

"Maybe he touched some squirrel poo and turned into a squirrel," Barnaby said, smirking. Nora frowned at him.

"Don't be gross. Mr. Hyde was just really brave," she said.

Isaac coughed. "Nora's right," he said. "In moments of extreme danger, people can exhibit extraordinary strength. Mothers have even been known to lift cars off their children —" He stopped and sniffed. "What's that smell?"

At the same moment, Jake saw an orange glow coming from Miss Jex. He could smell something too — a burning smell, like . . .

Burnt toast? In a flash, he realized.

"Miss Jex is changing! Everyone get down!"

Jake threw himself to the ground and covered his eyes.

FAAAAAAAAAAAAAARRRRRT!

Wheeeeeeeee . . . .

POP! POP! POP!

BANG!

Silence.

Jake lifted his head. Mr. Hyde was still standing at the foot of the tree. In his arms was Miss Jex, steaming a bit, but back to her normal, teachery self.

Miss Jex gazed up at Mr. Hyde. "Mr. Hyde! You rescued me. Even though you're scared of heights!"

Mr. Hyde's face went bright red. He hurriedly set her down and shook his head back and forth.

"It . . . it was nothing, Miss Jex," he mumbled. "Really!"

"No, it was brave," she said firmly. "I think that it was your bravery that changed me back into a human!"

Mr. Hyde went even deeper red.

"Miss Jex, you've got it wrong," he stammered. "It was my fault that you turned into a . . . a Creature. You see, I have this problem . . ."

"That wasn't your fault," Miss Jex said gently. "I must have inherited it from my mother. You see, she used to change into a Creature too."

Mr. Hyde gaped at Miss Jex. "Your mother?"

Miss Jex nodded. "I always thought it might happen to me one day. It must have been the electric shock from the stand's Van de Graaff generator that set me off. Funny — I've always had a thing about electricity!" She giggled at saying this, and then looked curiously at Mr. Hyde's head. "Excuse me, you seem to have a bird's nest in your hair." She reached out her hand."Let me . . ."

Watching the teachers, Jake suddenly gasped. He could have sworn he saw electric sparks fly between them as Miss Jex's hand touched Mr. Hyde's hair!

Jake looked closely at his teacher, and Mr. Hyde's face was definitely glowing.

"Oh no! He's changing again!" Jake started forward.

Nora pulled him back. "I don't think he's changing, Jake."

Jake looked at the two teachers. Miss Jex was glowing too! They looked like a pair of giant human-shaped glow sticks.

"So — why are they glowing, then?"

Nora rolled her eyes and drew a heart shape in the air. Jake's eyes widened.

"Ohh — *now* I get it!"

ABOUT THE AUTHOR

Sam Watkins voraciously consumed books from a young age, due to a food shortage in the village where she grew up. This diet, although not recommended by doctors, has given her a lifelong passion for books. She has been a bookseller, editor, and publisher, and writes and illustrates her own children's books. At one point, things all got a bit too bookish so she decided to be an art teacher for a while, but books won the day in the end.

ABOUT THE ILLUSTRATOR

David O'Connell is an illustrator who lives in London, England. His favorite things to draw are monsters, naughty children (another type of monster), batty old ladies, and evil cats . . . Oh, and teachers that transform into naughty little creatures!

GLOSSARY

antic (AN-tik) — a playful or funny act or action

clone (klohn) — an individual with identiclal genes to its parent

contradict (kahn-truh-DIKT) — to say the opposite of what has already been said

exhibit (ig-ZIB-it) — a public display of things that interest people

generator (JEN-uh-ray-tur) — a machine that produces electricity by turning a magnet inside a coil of wire

papier-mâché (PAY-pur-muh-SHAY) — paper that has been soaked in glue, which hardens when it dries

simulator (SIM-yuh-lay-tur) — a machine that allows you to experience under test conditions events similar to those likely to occur in a real situation

spawn (spawn) — the large number of eggs produced by amphibians like frogs

TALK ABOUT IT!

1. Do you have a pet? Would you want any of the creatures in this book for a pet? Discuss your answers with a friend.

2. Nora was surprised to hear Isaac call her the smartest person he knows. Talk about why you think she was surprised? Do you think his compliment changed anything in Nora?

3. After a day of chaos and messiness, the people at the science fair had a lot of cleaning up to do! Imagine a cool science project that could help put everything back in place. Would it be one gadget or would lots of people be able to help?

WRITE ABOUT IT!

1. Creature crosses with a frog, a spider, and an ant in the story! Think of another silly Creature combo. Write about the catalyst, what Creature would look like, and what his new abilities would be. When you're finished writing, draw a picture too!

2. Mr. Hyde is afraid of heights and Alexis is afraid of spiders. In the story, they both faced their fears to help someone else. Do you know what your best friends are afraid of? Write out three ways you could help your friends when they are afraid.

3. Mrs. Blunt and Amelia couldn't keep their secret about who truly made Rule-Bot. But what if they had kept it quiet? If you were in their shoes, what do you think it would feel like to win by cheating?

www.mycapstone.com